I0691888

Phebe Fuller McKeen

A Sketch of the Early Life of Joseph Hardy Neesima

Phebe Fuller McKeen

A Sketch of the Early Life of Joseph Hardy Neesima

ISBN/EAN: 9783337734190

Printed in Europe, USA, Canada, Australia, Japan

Cover: Foto ©Raphael Reischuk / pixelio.de

More available books at **www.hansebooks.com**

" Upright against God "

A SKETCH
OF THE EARLY LIFE OF
JOSEPH HARDY NEESIMA

BY
PHEBE FULLER McKEEN

Author of THORNTON HALL, THEODORA, AND LITTLE
MOTHER AND HER CHRISTMAS

WITH AN INTRODUCTION BY
PHILENA McKEEN

BOSTON
D LOTHROP COMPANY
WASHINGTON STREET OPPOSITE BROMFIELD

INTRODUCTION.

WHEN Joseph Neesima came, a stranger, to Andover in 1866, he attended — with the family where he had a pleasant home — the South Church, and there connected himself with a Sabbath School class of young men, taught by my sister, Miss Phebe Fuller McKeen.

This was the beginning of an intimate acquaintance. Mr. Neesima became our frequent and welcome visitor, and we were deeply interested in the snatches, thus incidentally caught, of his singular experience.

At my sister's request, he related to her,

7

at that time, the story of his life, which she immediately wrote out, that it might be on record, and largely in the charm of his own language. It could not have been published at that time without peril to interests political and social which were of great value both to himself and his family, and to his native land.

In the quickened feeling which the lamented death of Mr. Neesima excites, frequent requests have been made for the publication of this manuscript, the existence of which became known to a large circle. Friends of my sister will read it, longing

> " for the touch of a vanished hand,
> And the sound of a voice that is still."

This narrative will bring a crumb of comfort, as, weak in faith and sick at heart, we survey the heathen world; for by that Light which lighteth every man that cometh into the world, without the Word, or the voice of the preacher, one man renounced idolatry. With his first knowledge that, "in the beginning, God created the heaven and the earth," he gave his allegiance to his Creator. He had " the feelings of trust and reliance on God," which belong to sonship, long before he comprehended the mission of Christ as a Saviour. For months he had been in spiritual harmony with the Father without prayer, or being aware that he might pray, for he had not yet heard the wonderful announcement, " If ye shall ask anything of the Father, he will give it you in my name." Later, as he became acquainted with the gospels, he was deeply affected by the mediatorial office of Christ. Before me is his autograph card, upon the back of which, in his handwriting in Japanese characters, is a text which he said had been the central power in his Christian life. It was this: " For God so loved the world, that he gave his only begotten Son, that whosoever believeth in Him should not perish, but have everlasting life."

My sister's narrative closes with a petition which infolds a prophecy: the prayer has been answered, and the prophecy is remarkably fulfilled.

> " There's not a craving in the mind
> Thou dost not meet and still;
> There's not a wish the heart can have
> Which Thou dost not fulfill."

Under the kind patronage of Mr. and Mrs. Alpheus Hardy, his " American father and mother," Joseph Neesima went from Phillips Academy to Amherst College, and subsequently returned to Andover Theological Seminary, to prepare himself to preach the gospel to his people. Throughout his whole course of study, he was faithful, earnest and successful; although his environments were foreign, he easily distinguished himself among his American fellow students, for his heart was burning for his people, and he longed, as he said, " to be able to bring a light into the darkness."

Through a wonder-working Providence, as the time drew near when, having completed his studies, Mr. Neesima would be ready to return home, the Japanese Embassy came to this country, and Mr. Mori found in him a countryman eminently qualified to serve him as translator and aid. Together, in the interests of Japan, they visited the grand institutions of the United States, Great Britain, and the Continent, and, meanwhile, experienced mutually a growing respect and cordiality which threw a golden bridge over the chasm which lay between the self-exile and his home; furthermore, his connection with the Embassy gave him an advantageous introduction to his Government and her greatest statesmen.

It was his constant desire to found a school which should be a blessing to his country. He began with a half-dozen boys in a private house; at his death his Doshisha covers a group of schools where nearly a thousand students are taught in the preparatory, the collegiate, and the

MR. AND MRS. NEESIMA.

theological departments. There is also a training school for nurses, and special provision is made for the general education of young women as well as for young men in the Doshisha — the "One Purpose Society."

Such was Mr. Neesima's hold upon the confidence and affection of his people, that they made generous response to his appeals for help in the support of his Christian institution, which is now provided with several fine buildings.

He lived to welcome his parents and family into the household of faith, to enjoy a happy home of his own, where his tenderest sentiments and noblest ambitions were shared by his cultivated, Christian wife, to see his beloved Doshisha a remarkable success, and his country transformed by great moral, social and political changes. He was adored by his pupils, beloved by the missionaries associated with him, trusted by his government, honored by his Alma Mater with her highest academic degree, and held in affectionate remembrance by the multitude of his friends in America.

He died January 23, 1890, at Oiso, a health resort upon the coast; his remains reached Kyoto by the midnight train, and were received by hundreds of mourning students from the Doshisha, who lovingly bore them, with their own hands, to his home, two miles away.

On the succeeding Sabbath, memorial services were held both in Japanese and English, and warm tributes to his life and work were offered; more than three thou-

DORMITORIES CONNECTED WITH THE DOSHISHA.

sand were present at his obsequies and a funeral cortege reaching more than a mile in length followed his body to its resting-place. The students were again his bearers, and that as many as possible might share the coveted privilege of this last ministry to him whom they loved, the office was changed at short intervals.

His grave was made in the college burying-ground on a hillside overlooking the city and the surrounding plain. Students visit it as a shrine, and stimulate their spiritual life by his memory, and the hope that his mantle may fall upon them.

Mr. Neesima had been constantly true to his immediate conviction upon learning of God, " I belong to Heavenly Father, therefore I must believe Him and I must run in his way." The Father abundantly answered his earliest prayer: " Please let me reach my great aim."

It will be a rich contribution to biography and literature when Professor Arthur Sherburne Hardy shall publish his promised " Life of Dr. Joseph Hardy Neesima." Seldom has a biographer had so attractive a theme; and seldom is a theme treated by one so happily qualified by familiar acquaintance and warm personal friendship, by a feeling for perspective and values in portraiture, and by an obedient pen.

This brief sketch, written more than twenty years ago, must be read in the thought that it is a mere fragment; a fragment of a time when comparatively little was known of the life, religion, art and institutions of Japan, and long before Mr. Neesima achieved success as a student, a powerful speaker, a diplomatist, a man of extraordinary executive ability, and magnetism to draw about him a large circle of friends. It will be read with all the more interest because it is a sketch made at the time when God's purposes respecting him were all unknown, and those who were interested were praying that he might do what now they thank God for his having been permitted to accomplish. It is the story of the beginnings of a life which became ample and fruitful and conspicuous — worthy of an elaborate portrayal by a master hand.

P. McK.

Abbot Academy, Andover, Mass., 1890.

THE STORY OF NEESIMA.

THE STORY OF NEESIMA.

LESS than two years ago a young foreigner landed on our shores with a personal history so singular and suggestive that it deserves to be recorded. It shall be given, as far as is possible, in his own fresh English.

It was in the ancient city of Jeddo that Neesima first opened his eyes; and an odd-looking town he must have thought it, if babies were not such unbiased observers: black houses, paper front doors, and ladies carried along the streets in baskets. Strange, as the old woman said,

21

that folks can live so far off! Stranger still, what queer ways they do fall into, living there!

The family of Neesima belonged to the establishment of a Japanese prince, his grandfather being "officer of whole the prince's servants," and his father a sort of scribe or secretary to the same grandee. Still they lived by themselves in one of the houses connected with the palace. Funereal as all these buildings were externally, Neesima's home, at least, must have had a cheerful look inside, especially the family sitting-room; its papered walls hung with quaint pictures, and lined with wardrobes full of oriental garments — the floor hidden under heavy matting and trodden with unsandalled feet — the broad low window with its sliding sash of oiled

Joseph Nee-Sima.
約瑟 新島
Jeddo,
江戸
Japan.
日本

paper, half hidden in plants with their strange, rich blossoms — the bed of coals glowing in a large open brasier — the table, knee-high, in the middle of the room, strewn with curious writing utensils and corpulent little volumes in Japanese and Chinese with their silky leaves and elaborate letters — the sliding door of paper with the family cat, very likely, in the act of breaking through it. This was the room where most of Neesima's childish hours were spent. These little Japanese have a great advantage over our " wee bit toddlin' things," in the fact that grown people all sit on the floor, so that life is carried on at a level with their curious eyes.

As night falls, a strange transformation comes over this pleasant living-room. It is divided by screens into as many bed-rooms as are needed, mattresses are laid down, and each member of the family retires behind his screen, wraps the drapery of his couch about him in the shape of as many quilted wrappers as the weather demands, and lies down to pleasant dreams on a wooden pillow with a little cushion over it.

One feature of the sitting-room we have overlooked, which would be not only new, but sad to us. On a shelf against the wall stands a grim array of hideous gods, and among them are tablets inscribed with the names of dead ancestors. To all these the little Neesima was early taught by his father to pay homage, offering them rice and tea on a salver, and repeating forms of adoration. Before many years, however, the sturdy good sense of the boy protested against this absurd religion. For aught he knew, the whole world worshiped idols as devoutly as his father did; he had never heard of any other God, but he could see for himself that these were "only whittled out"; that they never touched the food and drinks he offered them, and that the oblation of wine set before them finally went down his father's throat; he was quite sure that he was better able to take care of himself than they were to take care of him, and from the time he was fifteen or sixteen years old, he could not be persuaded to pay the least respect to these helpless and senseless Penates.

So the boy grew up, sadly irreligious in his father's eyes, but fond of the saddle and the sword, active, studious and useful. The father kept in his house a little school for boys and girls — be it observed that girls are thought worth teaching in the Tycoon's dominions — and here Neesima first learned to read and write, and then helped to teach the rest. About the time he was sixteen years old, just as he had conceived a new zeal for books and was going into the study of Chinese with great enthusiasm, his "prince picked up him to write his daily book. Although it would not have been his desire, he was obliged to go up his office."

The Japanese nabobs think literary employments quite too laborious for royalty, and have most of their reading and writing, like every other kind of work, done for them. So Neesima took his place among some twenty clerks in his prince's office, sitting on the carpet around their low tables, tracing intricate, picture-like characters, with camel's hair pencils in India ink, as deftly as we can handle a pen. Laws were to be copied, facts recorded and letters written, at the prince's direction. By the way, these people have the fashion of superscribing their epistles with the name of the writer as well as the receiver.

Here the young scribe worked all day, and often far into the night, while shouts of revelry and the songs of dancing girls came from the banqueting hall of the palace. Every alternate day, however, he exchanged places with his father, and along with his "big sister" looked after the school at home. All the evenings at his disposal he gave to the study of Chinese.

But a new light dawned upon him which he shall describe in the rich simplicity of his own words:

" A day my comrade sent me a atlas of United States which was written in China-letter by some American minister. I read it many times and I was wondered so much as my brain would melted out from my head because I liked it very much — picking out president, building free school, poor-house, house of correction, and machine working and so forth. And I thought a governor of every country must be as President of United States, and murmured myself that O, governor of Japan! why you keep down us as a dog or pig? We are people of Japan; if you govern us you must love us as your children. From that time I wished to learn

LIBRARY OF THE DOSHISHA SCHOOL.

American knowledge, but alas! I could not get any teacher to learn it. Although I would not like to learn Holland, I was obliged to learn it, because many of my countrymen understood to read it."

Even for this second-best knowledge, it was difficult for him to find time and opportunity. Once when his prince had for the second time caught him running away from his office to go to his Dutch teacher, and had given him a flogging for it, he asked him, " Why you run out from here again ? "

" Then I answered to him," says Neesima, " I wish to learn foreign knowledge because foreigners have got best knowledge, and I hope to understand it very quickly; therefore, though I know I must stay here, reverence you low, my soul went to my master's house to learn it, and my body was obliged to go thither too. Then he said to me very kindly that 'You can write Japan very well and you can earn enough with it. If you don't run away from here any more, I will give you more wages. With what reason will you like foreign knowledge? Perhaps it will mistake yourself.'"

" I said to him sooner, 'Why will it mistake myself? I guess every one must take some knowledge. If a man has not any knowledge, I will worth him as a dog or pig!' Then he laughed very loud about it and said me, 'You are stable boy!'"

This was by no means the only time that the thirst for knowledge cost the boy both ridicule and blows. His family and acquaintances, as well as his prince, thought him very foolish to be craving needless knowledge; still he "never took care to them," and held "his counsel very fast." Business grew upon his hands, however, so that no time was to be had for study, and this cost him "many musings in his head," and at last made him fairly sick with thwarted purposes and unsatisfied longings. After various efforts to cure him, his physician had the good sense to tell him, "Your sickness comes from your mind, therefore you must try to destroy your warm mind and must take walks for the healthness of your body, and it would be more better than many medicine."

His prince gave him "plenty times to feed his weakness," and his father gave him some money to "play himself," all which he devoted to the ardent study of Dutch and "a small Book of Nature" which fell into his hands and delighted him so much that it proved "more better to his sickness than doctor's medicine."

So health came back, and with it came the busy days and studious nights. In his Book of Nature he met with some "reasonable accounts" which he was unable to understand, as it is thought unnecessary in Japan for boys to study arithmetic unless they are destined for trade. It was not his way to go over or around, but through, and as Lincoln laid down his book at the word "demonstration" and went through Euclid, this Japanese youth shut up his Natural History at the "reasonable accounts" and went to an arithmetic school until he had mastered the elementary principles of the science and could go through his book intelligently.

But here come some reflections of the young patriot in his own words.

"Some day I went to the seaside of Yeddo, hoping to see the view of the sea. I saw largest man-of-war of Dutch, laying there, and she seemed to me as a castle, or a battery, and I thought too that she would be strong enough to fight with enemy. While I look upon her, one reflection came upon my head, that we must open navy, because the country is surrounded by water, and if foreigners fight to my country we must fight with them at sea. But I made other reflection too, that since foreigners trade, price of everything get high, the country get poorer than before, because the country don't understand to do trade with foreigners. Therefore we must go to foreign countries, we must know to do trade, and we must learn foreign knowledge. But the Government's law neglected all my thoughts and I cried out myself:

"Why, Government? Why not let us be free? Why let us be as a bird in a cage or a rat within a bag? Nay, we must cast away such savage government. But alas! such things would have been out my power!"

So the solitary revolutionist shut up the cries of liberty within his own burning heart and patiently set to work in a government marine school whenever he could get away from his work, seeking information that he might turn to account for his country in the future.

He had just made a good beginning in navigation when night study injured his eyes, so that he was obliged to leave books entirely for a year and a half, "which would not come again in his life." He had hardly recovered from this trouble so as to resume his place in the prince's office when he was beset by measles, and his eyes, in consequence, " began to spoil again," so that he was forced "to spend many times very vainly."

When he did next use his eyes, however, it was to some purpose. " A day I visited my friend and I found out small Holy Bible in his library that was written by some American minister, with China language, and had shown only the most remarkable events of it. I lend it from him and read it at night. I was afraid the savage country's law which, if I read the Bible, Government will cross whole my family."

There were, at that time, three crimes in Japan for which crucifixion was the penalty; the murder of a master by a servant, a parent by his child, or the reading of the Bible!

This abridgment of the Bible contained little but the grand facts of creation and redemption, and these were entirely new to the earnest young soul that pored over its pages. It was indeed a Revelation to him.

"I put down the book and look around me, saying that 'Who made me — my parents? No! my God. Who made my table — a carpenter? No! my God; God let trees grow upon the earth. Although

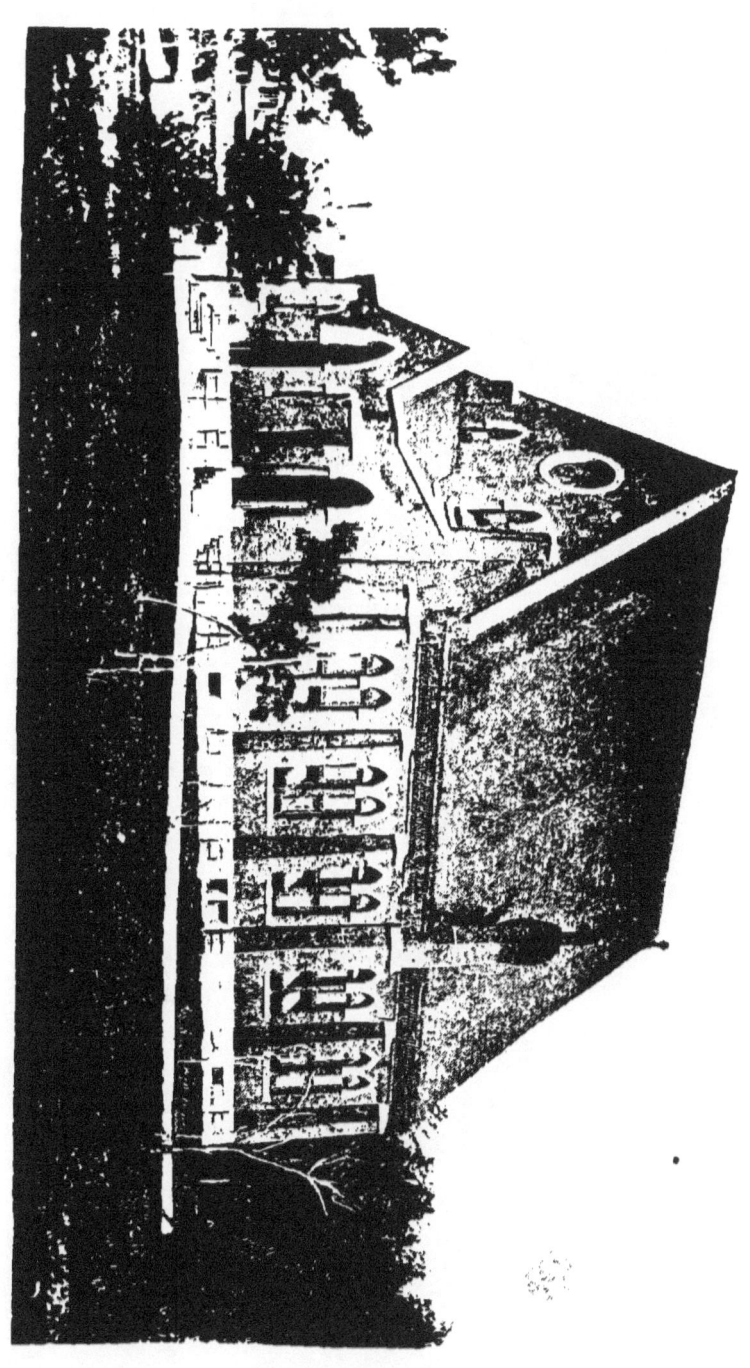

CHAPEL OF THE DOSHISHA SCHOOL.

the carpenter indeed made up this table it indeed came from trees.' Then I must be thankful to God; I must believe him, and I must be upright against him," was the swift and just conclusion.

So it was that without ever having seen one Christian believer, without one word of explanation from any human being, without the whole Bible even, this thoughtful, light-loving soul that had long scouted the gods of the heathen, recognized its eternal Father and fell at his feet in loving worship. Glorious old Revelation! Let it steal away from the tortures of its cold inquisitors and show itself only to the simple, truth-thirsty soul, it is hailed as the yearned-for Guide and Deliverer!

At once Neesima recognized, as it seems, his Maker's claim to love, trust and obedience, and began to yield them. It is a singular fact that it was more than a year before he learned that it is permitted to mortals to talk to this glorious Father as a man talketh with his friend. He "had the feeling," he says, "the feeling of trust and reliance on God," but the sweet possibility of prayer was not known to him.

From this time his "mind was fulfilled to read English Bible," and he burned to find some teacher or missionary who could instruct him and give him the whole word of God.

His father was, naturally enough, disturbed by his boy's new notions, and certain that he would get the whole family into trouble, and on asking permission of his prince and his parents to go to Hakodate, a port where he hoped to meet some Englishman or American, he got not only a refusal, but a flogging. Still his "stableness did not destroy by their expostulations." He next applied to the brother-in-law of his prince, a noble higher in rank and authority than he, and got leave from him to go in one of his own vessels to Hakodate. Having this sanction neither his prince nor his father was at liberty to prevent his going.

Not without pain, yet with a resolute heart, the young adventurer left the family in tears, and started on his search for truth, "no thinking that when money was gone how would he eat and dress himself," but only casting himself on the providence of God!

He had told his mother he thought he

would be gone a year, but at Hakodate he was doomed to disappointment. He sought in vain for any missionary or teacher of English. Meanwhile his small funds melted away very fast, and he was obliged to look about him to feed the outer man as well as the inner. He was more successful here, falling in with a Russian priest of the Greek church, who was glad to secure his services as teacher of Japanese. But, foiled in his great desire, he began to meditate leaving the country altogether. This idea the priest did his best to discourage, assuring him that he would teach him all he needed to know. On the other hand, he was warmly encouraged to go by three or four of his countrymen, whose acquaintance he had made at his hotel. Indeed, Neesima says there is a strong inclination among the young men of Japan to visit foreign lands, which nothing but the severity of the Government, and the hostages given it in wife and children, holds in check. The more he saw of his native island the more indignant he became at the tyranny that oppressed it; he "felt injured," and he longed to be able to "bring a light into the darkness."

Still, it was a very serious question; if he left the country, death would be his only welcome back. To go, was to adventure himself, a penniless exile, with an unknown tongue, into a new, mysterious world, of which he only knew that truth was there; more than all, it was to bring grief and fear, possibly danger, into the home he loved. "But one reflection," he says, "came upon my head, that although my parents fed me, I belong indeed to Heavenly Father. Therefore I must believe him, and I must run in his way." Remember he had never yet seen a Christian. "Then I began to search some vessel to get out from the country."

A kind helper in this undertaking was one of his new friends, a young Japanese in charge of an English store and understanding the language well. He secured a passage for him in an American schooner bound for Shanghai. It was necessary to get away as secretly as possible. The eventful night came. The voyager met his three friends for the last time. The cup of rice wine was passed from lip to lip in pledge of friendship. They all wished they were going too, cheered him on, and bade him good-by. One of them — the clerk — promised to have a boat waiting at the water's edge near his store, at twelve o'clock, to take him to the schooner, though Neesima was as much in dread of compromising this faithful friend as of betraying himself.

At midnight a whispered word of parting, hushed footsteps, the muffled dip of oars, and the true-hearted young patriot, who went to seek light and blessing for his country even more than himself, had stolen out from its shores like a culprit. This was on the eighteenth of July, 1864.

After a disagreeable passage to China, and ten days of waiting in constant anxiety, lest by some treachery he should be spirited back to Japan, he had the happiness of finding an American vessel bound for

Boston. By means of a Japanese-English dictionary he succeeded in making the captain understand that he would be glad to do anything, and ask no other pay than to be taken to America, and "begged to him, if I get to America, please let me go to a school and let me take good education."

So the kind-hearted Yankee captain took him as his own attendant, dressed him in Frank costume, gave him a Christian name, and on the voyage taught him navigation and English.

The voyage was a long and roundabout way to the goal of his most ardent wishes. The Wild Rover traded along the coast of China for eight months, before turning her prow towards the New World. While they lay in the harbor of Hong Kong,

Neesima found the New Testament in Chinese; he must have it, but how should he get it, since he had promised to ask for no money? At last he joyfully bethought himself of a piece of property that he might exchange for it; the young gentlemen of Yeddo wear two swords, a short and a long one; so our hero sold his rapier to the captain and became, for the first time, the rich possessor of a whole New Testament.

At length sails were set for the West, and in four months from that time the land of promise dawned upon our wanderer. Even then it seemed as if he was to be baffled. Directly after coming into port at Boston, his protector, the captain, went to the Cape to see his friends, and for ten weeks Neesima was left to "rough and godless men, who kept the ship," doing hard, heavy work, such as he had never been accustomed to. Besides, everybody on the wharf frightened him. They told him " Nobody on the shore will relieve you, because since the war the price of everything got high. Ah, you must go to sea again." " I thought too," he says, " that I must work pretty well for my eating and dressing, and I could not get in any school before I could earn any money to pay to a school. When such thoughts pressed my brain, I could not work very well; I could not read book very cheerfully, and only looked around myself long time as a lunatic."

One great discovery, however, he had already made. The captain had given him a little money to amuse himself with on shore, and he had treated himself to a Robinson Crusoe, which he found at some bookstore on Washington Street, and Robinson Crusoe first taught him that he might pray! His New Testament in a foreign language he had not yet entirely mastered. This shipwrecked Robinson Crusoe prayed in his distress; why might not he? So every night after he went to bed he "prayed to the God, ' Please don't cast me away into miserable condition: please let me reach my great aim.' "

Ah, how little we know when we pray, how long our Father has been preparing to answer our prayer! That God who had turned the boy's heart from idols, who had inspired him to feel after Him, if haply he might find him, who had said unto him, " Get thee out of thy country and from thy kindred and from thy father's house, into the land which I will show thee,"— He had not neglected, we may be sure, to prepare a place for him. He had brought the young wanderer across the seas in a ship belonging to one of His own children, straight to the hands of one whose joy it was to spend his strength and his wealth in the service of his beloved Lord. On learning from the captain the story of his protégé, this Christian ship-owner gladly accepted the trust thus sent him from the other side of the world, and took upon himself at once the whole charge of the young stranger's support and education.

"When I first heard these things from my captain," said Neesima, "I jumped for joy, my eyes was fulfilled with many tears because I was very thankful to him, and I thought, too, God will not forsake me !"

By his patron, Hon. Alpheus Hardy of Boston, he was immediately put at Phillips Academy, Andover, where he has been now a little more than a year. " His desire is fulfilled; he takes good education." In the crowd of young American students about him, he finds, as his teachers say, no superior in intellect. His mind has an indomitable propensity for diving to the bottom.

On the last Sabbath of 1866 Neesima was received as a brother beloved into the church of the First-born, and welcomed to the Table of the Lord, in the chapel of the Andover Seminary. It was a long time after he had begun to " be thankful to God, believe Him, and be upright against Him," that he comprehended the mission of Christ. He had not thought of himself as a sinner, but as he read on, and found out the high, pure morality and religion of the Bible, he condemned himself, and, as a sinner, laid hold upon the Saviour. He had not known sin but by the law, yet it was a blessed law which brought a gospel with it.

Such is the account prepared very soon after Neesima's arrival in this country, and chiefly in his own English, before it was run in the ordinary moulds of the more correct language which he now uses. Every particular of this story is strictly true. When permission was asked to publish his history, he declined, saying he " was not worth it, and he did not like to be made public." But upon the suggestion that, as a fresh proof of the power of the Bible and of God's beautiful providence, it might be useful to others, he cheerfully consented, only stipulating that his real name and present place of residence be withheld; in fact this was a matter of prudence as well as of preference. Nothing could be more repugnant to him than to be made an object of indifferent curiosity. From his school-fellows and teachers and the kind Christian family where he always boarded in Andover, he is accustomed to receive unqualified respect and affection. Enough cannot be said of his character and ability, without wronging a modesty and simplicity of heart which are to be revered.

It is still his great hope and purpose to

do something for his countrymen. Although under a strict interpretation of Japanese law he would be liable to execution if he should return to Japan, by the time he is ready for work he will have a right to claim, should he desire it, the protection of the American flag, and it may be hoped also that his Government will have made progress in liberal ideas. May God permit him to bestow on his beloved island the sacred treasures he has found in his world-wide quest!

And may God rouse in us a deeper sympathy for the noble souls that are pining in darkness for the light!

P. F. McK.

ABBOT ACADEMY, Andover, Mass., 1867.